THE CHIMPANZEES' HAPPY TREE

For Victoria, who makes our lives a Happytown – G.A.

For my wonderful agent, Hilary – G.P-R.

ORCHARD BOOKS
First published as *The Chimpanzees of Happy Town* in 2006 by The Watts Publishing Group
This revised edition published as *The Chimpanzees' Happy Tree* in 2021

1 3 5 7 9 10 8 6 4 2

Text © Giles Andreae, 2006, 2021
Illustrations © Guy Parker-Rees, 2006

ISBN 978 1 40836 689 9

Printed in the UK

Orchard Books
An imprint of Hachette Children's Group
Part of The Watts Publishing Group Limited
Carmelite House, 50 Victoria Embankment
London EC4Y 0DZ

An Hachette UK Company
www.hachette.co.uk
www.hachettechildrens.co.uk

ORCHARD

THE CHIMPANZEES' HAPPY TREE

GILES ANDREAE

GUY PARKER-REES

Drabsville was a rainy town
Not very far away,
Where all the houses looked the same
And all of them were grey.

There were **no** parks to play in,

No grass, **no** trees at all.

And the chimpanzees who lived there
All felt very **sad** and **small**.

Then one day, Chutney came back home.
He'd travelled far and wide.
And with him was a precious box,
Which held a seed inside.

"I'm going to plant this here," he said,
"And let it blossom **free**,
Because, my friends, this seed is from
A special Happy Tree!"

He fed it

and he watered it,

And watched it slowly grow,
But from way up in his palace
The mayor boomed,
"No, no, no!"

"You **don't** grow trees in **Drabsville!**
We can't have things that flower.
Chutney, I'm afraid I'll have to
lock you in the tower!"

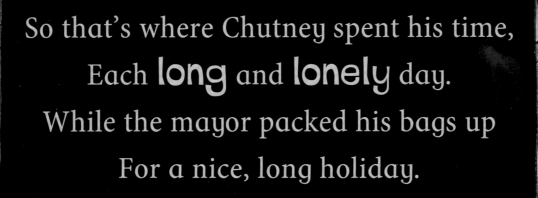

So that's where Chutney spent his time,
Each **long** and **lonely** day.
While the mayor packed his bags up
For a nice, long holiday.

Meanwhile, back at
Chutney's house,

The boy and girl next door
Said, "We **must** water Chutney's seed
And make it grow some **more!**"

And, as the tree began to **blossom**,
Just like Chutney said,
The children both began to feel
The **happiness** it spread.

And Chutney, from his lonely tower,
Looked out one day to see
The **leaves** and **flowers** and **branches**
Of his own beloved tree.

And when, at last, they let him out
He said, "It's time to show

You just **can't** keep down **happiness**.
You need to let it **grow!**"

"Let's make our houses

colourful.

Let's pull our fences down.

And, chimpanzees, let's change

This place's name to . . .

HAPPYTOWN!"

"I'll paint mine **pink!**" one voice replied.
"That's what I'm going to do.

Then I'm going to climb up on the roof

And paint the chimney **blue!**

My windows will look **fabulous**
Without those iron bars.
And the walls will be a symphony
Of **flowers** and **hearts** and **stars!**"

Then Chutney stopped and looked up
At the palace of the mayor.
"The children need a place to play,"
He said. "Let's build it there."

So in the palace grounds, they built
A playground with some **swings**,

A **roundabout**,

a **rocket ship**,

And **loads** of other things.

"Let's have a party," Chutney said,
"With yummy things to eat!"
There were sausages and ice cream.
There was dancing in the street.

"Hooray for Chutney!"

someone cheered,

And everyone agreed.

Except the mayor,
who came home,

And was **very**
cross indeed.

He didn't want to join them
So they took him to the tower.

Then one day Chutney
gave the mayor
A little **Happy Flower**.

"I brought this from my tree," he said,
"And look – it goes to show
That **happiness** will **always** find
Its own true way to grow."

"Yes, things will **always** blossom
If we dare to set them **free**.

It's no different for a little flower
As for a chimpanzee."